JOURNEY TO THE CENTER OF THE EARTH 3D

JOURNAL FROM THE CENTER OF THE EARTH

D1044463

Adapted by E. Mason

Based on the screenplay by Michael Weiss
and Jennifer Flackett & Mark Levin

PSS!
PRICE STERN SLOAN

PRICE STERN SLOAN
Published by the Penguin Group
Penguin Group (USA) Inc., 375 Hudson Street, New York, New York 10014, USA
Penguin Group (Canada), 90 Eglinton Avenue East, Suite 700,
Toronto, Ontario M4P 2Y3, Canada
(a division of Pearson Penguin Canada Inc.)
Penguin Books Ltd., 80 Strand, London WC2R 0RL, England
Penguin Group Ireland, 25 St. Stephen's Green, Dublin 2, Ireland
(a division of Penguin Books Ltd.)
Penguin Group (Australia), 250 Camberwell Road, Camberwell, Victoria 3124, Australia
(a division of Pearson Australia Group Pty. Ltd.)
Penguin Books India Pvt. Ltd., 11 Community Centre, Panchsheel Park,
New Delhi—110 017, India
Penguin Group (NZ), 67 Apollo Drive, Rosedale, North Shore 0632, New Zealand
(a division of Pearson New Zealand Ltd.)
Penguin Books (South Africa) (Pty.) Ltd., 24 Sturdee Avenue,
Rosebank, Johannesburg 2196, South Africa

Penguin Books Ltd., Registered Offices:
80 Strand, London WC2R 0RL, England

The scanning, uploading, and distribution of this book via the Internet or via any other
means without the permission of the publisher is illegal and punishable by law. Please
purchase only authorized electronic editions and do not participate in or encourage
electronic piracy of copyrighted materials. Your support of the author's rights is appreciated.

©MMVIII New Line Productions, Inc./ Walden Media, LLC. Journey to the Center of the
Earth™, Journey to the Center of the Earth 3D™ and all characters, places, names and
other indicia are trademarks of New Line Productions, Inc. and Walden Media, LLC. All
Rights Reserved. www.walden.com/journey3d. www.journey3dmovie.com. Used under
license by Penguin Young Readers Group. All rights reserved. Published by Price Stern
Sloan, a division of Penguin Young Readers Group, 345 Hudson Street, New York, New York
10014. PSS! is a registered trademark of Penguin Group (USA) Inc. Printed in the U.S.A.

The publisher does not have any control over and does not assume any responsibility for
author or third-party websites or their content.

Library of Congress Control Number: 2007046217

ISBN 978-0-8431-3231-1   10 9 8 7 6 5 4 3 2 1

This is the field journal of SEAN ANDERSON. This is not a diary. Diaries are for girls. Diaries come with sparkle pens and have tiny little locks on the outside that you can pick EASILY with a screwdriver. Ever tried that? Works like a charm.

I repeat: This is <u>NOT A DIARY</u>. Does it look like I'm writing with a sparkle pen?

Just wanted to make that clear.

Scientists keep field journals. You know, when they're studying bugs or rocks or jellyfish or whatever. It's way more interesting than it sounds.

Plus, my dad kept a field journal. He was a scientist. I guess you could say it runs in the family. So . . .

~~Keep out~~
~~Read At Your own Risk~~
Who cares?
Turn the page. I <u>dare you.</u>

First, This Might Sound Crazy...

I was gonna write about my dad. But first, here's some choice info about me:

NAME: SEAN ANDERSON

AGE: 13

FROM: used to be: Orange, NJ
now: Ottawa, Canada

SKILLZ: Video game master
Skateboarding
Yo-yo guru (getting there)
Mountain-climbing
Kite-flying
Dinosaur-dodging (no joke)
Diamond-hunting
And not ashamed to be a Vernian! (more on that soon)

About my dad: His name was Max. Maxwell Anderson. First off, he's not around anymore. He died when I was little, so I didn't really know the guy. But don't feel sorry for me. You have no clue what a cool guy my dad was. Not yet anyway.

The second thing about him is that he was a major scientist. He studied something called plate tectonics. That's a theory that the Earth's surface is made up of all these big plates that are constantly moving and shifting and overlapping. Less than a week ago I had the TIME OF MY LIFE and it was all sorta thanks to my dad. And my uncle Trevor. And an Icelandic mountain guide named Hannah. And this guy named Jules Verne.

My dad thought this book (by Jules Verne) was the real deal:

Not science fiction ↓

JOURNEY TO THE CENTER OF THE EARTH

Because of this book, my dad believed there was a whole world under the Earth's crust. That you could climb down through a volcano and walk around underground. Down there in the center of the Earth, you'd see trees. And sky. And rivers. And even dinosaurs. <u>YES</u>. Dinosaurs still exist, down where people can't see them.

I bet that sounds crazy. If anyone was reading this (and I don't care if you are), I bet they'd think I'm having some weird dream, like the one where you're suddenly able to fly over your school and you've got X-ray vision so you can see through the roof into the cafeteria where the lunch lady is putting dog food in the sloppy joes (just like you suspected!) and you swoop down and zap the sloppy joes out of the cafeteria with laser beams so everyone can have pizza instead, and then you skip class and just fly around for a while 'cause you can.

You know those dreams.
EVERYBODY has those dreams. (Don't they?)

Anyway, people thought my dad's theories about the center of the Earth and Jules Verne's book being real were nuts. And when my dad disappeared, no one EVER thought he made it down there.

They were wrong. Dead wrong.
            And I, Sean Anderson, have got the proof.

Now About Uncle Trevor...

It all started with a lame trip (so I thought) to stay with my nerdy Uncle Trevor.

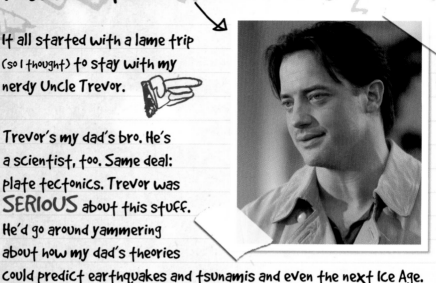

Trevor's my dad's bro. He's a scientist, too. Same deal: plate tectonics. Trevor was **SERIOUS** about this stuff. He'd go around yammering about how my dad's theories could predict earthquakes and tsunamis and even the next Ice Age.

(You know what I think of when I hear the words ICE AGE? Woolly mammoths. And I can't help but laugh, even though it's not that funny. because we don't want the planet to freeze up like a snowball.)

EXPLORATION:
OBSERVATIONS DAY 2, JULY 2

DANGER:
Albino Gigantosaurus

ENTRA
MT.

But woolly mammoths? Big fat furry elephants with those crazy huge tusks? Who wouldn't want to have a bunch of those hairy dudes still wandering around? Extinction sucks. If they were still around, I'd want to go on a woolly mammoth safari. I would pet one if it let me, and I'd feed it peanuts, maybe. I wouldn't ride one, though. I think it'd be way too cruel to ride a woolly mammoth. I once rode an elephant at the fair and the poor guy seemed so mopey with all these kids climbing on him, so yeah: Don't ride the elephants. It's just wrong. What I want to ride is a scooter. Or a Jet Ski. I'm gonna ask for one for my birthday.)

Back to Trevor.

I'm guessing he wasn't expecting me. The place was a total mess. Mom would've BUGGED OUT if she had seen it, but she had to run to find us a new house in Ottawa (that's in canada), so it was just Trevor and me. I thought I'd be bored out of my mind. That's not exactly what happened.

"Nature Abhors a Vacuum."

← Uncle Trevor said that.

I guess when you're a genius you don't have time to clean. It's hard to have deep thoughts when you're scrubbing grimy pots and sorting socks. ~~If~~ When I am a genius scientist, I'll just invent something to clean for me. Like a <u>gravity-defying magnetic dust mop</u>

that sorts laundry and isn't afraid to unclog the toilet. GENIUS. In the meantime, my mom just makes me clean my room the old-fashioned way. She says it builds character. I say it's a waste of time.

Mom

Anyway, there was this box. My mom gave it to Trevor. In it was my dad's stuff: books, papers, pictures. (Most of the pictures were of Trevor and my dad. Trevor said they were partners in crime. Wish I could've seen <u>that</u>.)

More pictures. More papers. And—score!—a yo-yo.* Hey, I needed SOMETHING to keep me entertained.

* Trevor says this yo-yo was what my dad did instead of playing video games. Kinda cool.

7

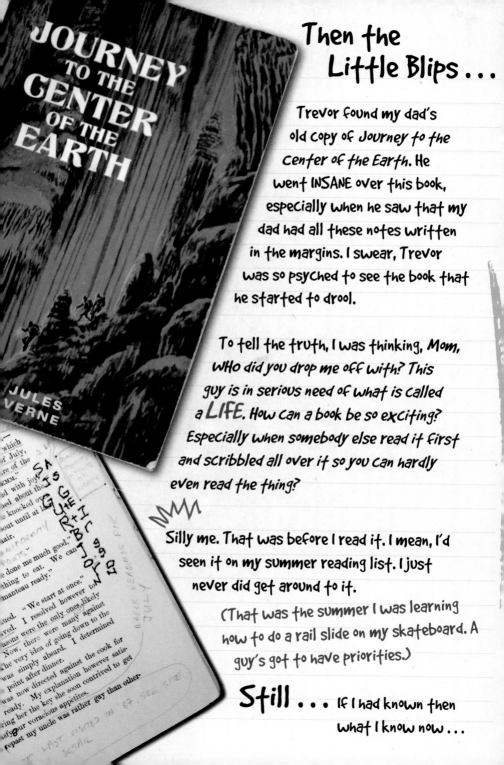

Then the Little Blips...

Trevor found my dad's
old copy of Journey to the
Center of the Earth. He
went INSANE over this book,
especially when he saw that my
dad had all these notes written
in the margins. I swear, Trevor
was so psyched to see the book that
he started to drool.

To tell the truth, I was thinking, Mom,
WHO did you drop me off with? This
guy is in serious need of what is called
a **LIFE**. How can a book be so exciting?
Especially when somebody else read it first
and scribbled all over it so you can hardly
even read the thing?

Silly me. That was before I read it. I mean, I'd
seen it on my summer reading list. I just
never did get around to it.

(That was the summer I was learning
how to do a rail slide on my skateboard. A
guy's got to have priorities.)

Still... If I had known then what I know now...

Well, let's just say I would've left the skateboard alone for a couple days and caught up on my reading.

So after we looked through the box, Trevor wanted to show me his science lab. Really he just wanted to check into some science mumbo jumbo he had found in my dad's notes. He was blabbering on about tectonophysics being the science of now, whatever that means. He was going wild over some numbers. What a snore, right?   Sort of. At first.

Then he told me that conditions all over the world were just like they were in July 1997. When dad disappeared.

Then Trevor showed me these little blips on a computer map of the world. One blip. Two blips. Three blips. Four blips.

Trevor said they were my dad's seismic sensors. It was how they monitored Earth's vibrations, like earthquakes, all over the world. And he said there were only _three_ blips. Dude, like I don't know how to count. I pointed out: FOUR BLIPS. Was he blind? And that fourth blip was blipping like a maniac. No one could miss it.

Trevor was thrilled. That fourth and most important blip was over Iceland.

That's Right.
Iceland. →

Iceland is an island that sits far, far up north in the Atlantic ocean, somewhere between the top of Europe and Greenland.

Now if someone told me my uncle would take me for a trip to some faraway island, I'd figure we'd be heading to Maui, maybe. You know, scuba diving, surfing lessons, kicking it on the beach.

Not a chance. We were going to Iceland to find that seismic sensor. At first, he thought he could ship me back to my mom. Of course, I talked him out of it. What else was Trevor gonna do with his giant coin collection (FOUR JARS) except splurge on two plane tickets?

Next thing I knew, we were in a plane on our way to Iceland. It's all in the name: Ice. Land. So, yeah, I packed a jacket.

(BTW, my dad had written these two weird words in the margins of *Journey to the Center of the Earth*. Sigurbjörn Asgeirsson, it said. Trevor was doing word puzzles trying to figure out what they meant until he finally found an address on the last page of the book for a place called the Ásgeirsson Institute for Progressive Volcanology. We figured this Sigurbjörn dude must run the place ... and my dad must have been in touch with him before he disappeared.)

sigurbjörn asgeirsson

10

Are We There Yet?

We landed in Iceland. First impression? This island sure does get some snow.

So we bundled up, rented a car, and hit the road.

There's no point in describing the driving part except to say we were in THE ABSOLUTE MIDDLE OF NOWHERE, and Uncle Trevor was driving that car so agonizingly slowly through the snow that I saw a goat pass us on the road. Seriously!

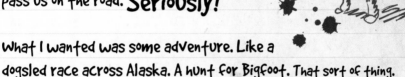

What I wanted was some adventure. Like a dogsled race across Alaska. A hunt for Bigfoot. That sort of thing.

But Uncle Trevor's idea of adventure was finding this Institute place. When we found it (there was so much snow Trevor almost drove INTo it), I gotta say, it wasn't what I was expecting.

It was this tiny little shack. It reminded me of the outhouse at my summer camp.

Actually I think the outhouse was bigger.

Progressive Volcanology & the Eight-Track Tape

This is what we learned when we stood outside the ~~outhouse~~ institute waiting for the Icelandic woman to let us in: →

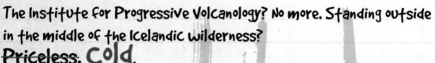

Sigurbjörn Ásgeirsson? Dead and gone.

The Institute for Progressive Volcanology? No more. Standing outside in the middle of the Icelandic wilderness? ~~Priceless.~~ Cold.

The woman's name was **Hannah.** Turns out that Sigurbjörn Ásgeirsson was her dad. She didn't believe in his theories, though. She said progressive volcanology was a failed idea. Like the Berlin Wall. or the eight-track tape.*

* Eight-track tapes were these big honking monster tapes people used to play music on way before CDs were invented. The tapes weighed fifty pounds each and could only hold one song at a time, and you needed a stereo the size of a refrigerator to play them. That's sad. And I used to feel bad for people who still use record players.

Hannah sure did not think too much of this progressive volcanology stuff.

My uncle was a little hurt. It was like she had broken the news that there was no Santa Claus. Now I know there's no Santa Claus (I have known since I was five and spied my mom snarfing down his plate of cookies), but I had to think of Trevor. The dude's a believer.

Five Signs That You're a Vernian

Hannah called her dad a **"Vernian."** That's a member of La Société de Jules Verne (that's French for "The Society of Jules Verne"). These people believe that **Jules Verne's writing is real,** even though his books are called science fiction. Vernians call Jules Verne a **visionary.**

But Hannah sure didn't think so. "A Vernian is a fool" is what Hannah said. (Soon she'll wish she had never said that, but I'm not there yet.)

How to know if you're a Vernian:

1) Your copy of **Journey to the Center of the Earth** looks like your dog used it for a game of fetch.

2) You do not think **"Snaeffels"** is the sound someone with a runny nose makes.

3) You'd hop on a plane to Iceland just because you saw some blip blipping and you must know why.

4) You find yourself in Iceland. At the top of the mountain. On the first of July. (And you know why that day matters.)

5) You're not ashamed when someone calls you a Vernian. **Vernians rule!**

(I got all five after our trip. Who's the fool now?)

Now for Some Adventure

Turns out Hannah was a professional mountain guide. So when she heard we were heading off to find a seismic sensor on top of some mountain, she said she'd lead us there. ~~If~~ Uncle Trevor paid her. (Thankfully, he did.) (And, more thankfully, she accepted rolls of quarters.)

So I was thinking we'd follow Hannah up some **nice mountain path**, not too fast, not too slow, stop to **warm** our hands by a fire, roast a couple marshmallows . . . right? **I mean, don't Icelandic mountain guides like marshmallows? Guess not.**

As we crossed the tundra I could barely recognize myself. **Back in New Jersey, I could shoot hoops, grab a skateboard and do a few tricks, then ride my bike home without breaking a sweat.** No problemo.

But in Rvvvvsjkskssjsjggkkkkvk (or something like that), Iceland, I needed an oxygen tank just to keep up.

Note to self: Next time do some push-ups first.

ENTRANCE POINT
MT. SNAEFFELS

MAXWELL
CENTER FOR THE
STUDY OF
PLATE TECTONICS
ANDERSON

Temperatures exceed 120°F

Glowbird sightings

on Top of old Snaeffels

We ended up on some mountain peak called **Snaeffels** (no joke; that's the name). In the Jules Verne book, Snaeffels was where the **character Lidenbrock** supposedly found a portal to the center of the Earth. And to top it all off, it turned out that he found this so-called portal on July 1. Jules Verne called that the kalends of July.

Guess what day we climbed Mt. Snaeffels? July 1. **Yep**, the kalends.

Dude.

Check this out:

. . . in the center of the Jokul of Snaeffels when the shadow of Scartaris touches, at the kalends of July, you will attain the center of the Earth . . .

What does that mean in, like, English?

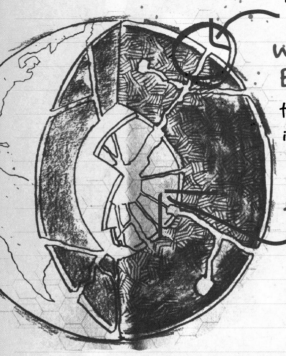

That means if you stand on the spot WHERE WE WERE STANDING on the EXACT DAY we were there, some hole will open up in the ground and if you slip into it you'll fall down to

THE CENTER OF THE EARTH.

Supposedly.

That's what I was thinking at the time. I admit it. BUT one look at Uncle Trevor and I knew he really believed in it. Snaeffels or no Snaeffels, I had a feeling something big was about to happen.

Still, when we found the seismic sensor, it was blinking red, and even though it started raining Trevor ran straight for it. I didn't think it would happen <u>right away</u>.

What NOT to Do in a Lightning Storm

(Lessons learned, thanks to Uncle Trevor.)

So if you happen to find yourself on top of a mountain with thunder crashing and lightning flashing and there's so much rain you can't see straight . . .

do NOT, I repeat,

DO NOT:

1. Just stand there in the rain.

2. Run back and forth in the rain.

3. Run back and forth in the rain while waving an electronic device that's attracting all the lightning.

So yeah. Uncle Trevor braved the storm to get the seismic sensor. As for me and Hannah, we were smart. We took cover in a cave.

There's <u>Always</u> Another Way.

That was some storm. Uncle Trevor jumped into the cave just in time. Then the entrance to the cave collapsed and trapped us inside. One second it's the way out, the next second it's a wall of rocks on top of rocks on top of rocks. On top of, yep, more rocks.

Trevor said it would've taken us six months to dig through it. SIX MONTHS.

Maybe I panicked a little. Being trapped in a cave for six months would do that to anyone. Totally natural reaction.

Then at some point I remember Hannah turning to me and saying, "<u>There's always another way.</u>" So I had to trust her. I mean, it's not like I haven't been trapped in some bad spots before. Try sitting through Mr. Ianotti's social studies class.

I'm just sayin'.

Anyway, up in that cave I wasn't exactly thinking straight. I tried my cell phone. No signal. Um, duh. Guess when you're buried under magnetically charged rocks in the middle of nowhere, you can expect your service to be spotty.

I thought of my mom. Uncle Trevor said he had promised her he'd take care of me. Some promise.

I mean, right at that moment Mom was probably driving down some road in Ottawa, on the way to look at one house or another, trying to figure out where we'd live. *What side of the road do they drive on in Canada?* I was thinking. *The right or the left?** I couldn't remember. Somehow it calmed me down, just thinking: *Right or left? Right or left? Right or left? I have to get outta this cave,* I told myself, *and I'll make it to Canada and I'll find out.*

Sounds silly now. But it worked. Hannah turned on the flashlights and led the way.

*The right side. It's not England.

Keep out . . .
or Not.

Trevor said he had a sixth sense about direction. Some sixth sense: It led us straight to a dead end.

Turns out what we were wandering around inside wasn't a normal mountain—it was a **VOLCANO**. One of those things full of boiling lava that tends to explode and bury whole cities. I mean, where was all the lava hiding? <u>Somewhere.</u>

The way out wasn't so easy to find. No doorway marked EXIT like at the movie theater. The one sign we found was in Icelandic. **KEEP OUT**, the sign said. The area we were supposed to keep out of was an old abandoned mine. Hannah said maybe that way would lead us to the mineshaft. So that's where we went.

We used ropes to climb deep down into this long tunnel. Trevor got all psyched about the rocks—so excited that at one point he almost fell in, but Hannah caught him.

As for me, I got distracted. I was looking down. There was just this darkness, this **NOTHINGNESS.**

I have never seen so much nothing in my whole entire life.

I was wondering if that was the way into the center of the Earth. It looked like twelve football fields of nothing: no stars, no lights. I felt real small standing there over that hole.

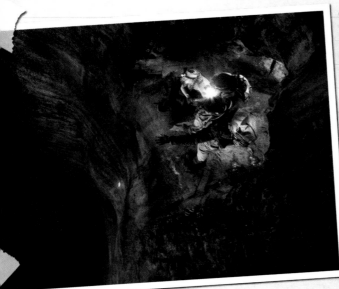

Of course, Trevor got this idea that he had to SEE the nothing. So he lit a flare. The light was fiery red at first, but then Trevor accidentally touched the flare to the rock wall behind him . . .

 **BOOM.**   It exploded in <u>white fire.</u>

Uncle Trevor the genius, at it again. By almost blowing us up, he figured out that the rock in the wall was magnesium. Which is kind of flammable. Like, so flammable it's used to make gunpowder.

So we learned not to trust Uncle Trevor with the flares.

Really long, long way down.

In My DNA

After Trevor messed up with the flare, we had to use a glow stick. We watched it fall down into the chasm. I got hung up on the word: CHASM. Nothing good can come from jumping into a chasm. You can just tell by the way it sounds.

I timed the glow stick's fall on my watch. One long second. Two. Three.

Then we heard it go CLUNK really far down below. Three seconds to the bottom is good, right? Not so much. Technically, that meant the vertical chasm was two hundred feet long.

You know, your basic twenty-story high rise.

Um, yeah . . .

We went rappelling down into the hole on ropes. I'll be honest. For a minute there, I was gonna stay up top. I mean, why go down in the first place? Chasm. Enough said. But Trevor talked me into it. **He said climbing is in my DNA.**

He meant my dad. The guy who explored the world, who wasn't afraid of anything. Dad was an expert climber—mountain peaks, you name it. Mom didn't like to talk about him, but I knew enough. If climbing down into chasms is in my DNA, who knows what else I got from Dad? Maybe I can fly, too. Here's hoping.

I'll try to describe what rappelling down into total darkness is like. You're hanging on by a thread (okay, call it a rope, same difference). And below you there's what looks like this: ~~███████~~

I couldn't see where we were going. Understatement.
I could hardly even see when Trevor fell down too far, almost pulling us down with him. It was either us or him. Hannah cut the rope. She said she had to do it.

Heartless? Maybe.

Except the bottom was, like, eighteen inches away. He landed with a thump on his butt. No harm, no foul.

What If?

So the chasm did have a bottom. I figured as much. I mean, what chasm doesn't have a bottom? It's not like you could just be walking down the street and trip over the curb and fall into a manhole and just keep falling until you fell out the other side of the planet. That kind of thing does not happen. In real life when you fall, you hit ground.

But, seeing as my real life didn't used to include running around inside volcanoes, I wasn't about to say something was impossible.

Down there at the bottom of that chasm was this old abandoned mine. The place was creepy. It got shut down sixty years ago after some big disaster. Part of me wanted to yell out into the empty caverns to hear my voice echo back. Another part wanted to just keep quiet and keep walking till we made it out.
(Ghosts and all.)

I sort of hung back and kept to myself while my uncle and Hannah got to talking. I was thinking about Hannah's dad. I had heard her say he died in an insane asylum, still raving about the center of the Earth. And that got me thinking about my own dad.

I was thinking, what if he was right? I mean, *WHAT IF?*

I was about to find out.

Roller coaster!

Inside that mine was Iceland's best-kept secret: this huge cavern filled with train tracks leading in every possible direction you could think of. Those tracks twisted, turned, flipped, circled, and swooped through the air just the way I like 'em. There were old mining cars on the tracks, too. Sure, the people who once worked the mines probably used the cars and the tracks to cart rocks around. But when I saw the setup, my first thought was:

(Maybe that was my second thought. My first thought was: FINALLY, we found a way out. The miners had to cart stuff out of this volcano, so the tracks must lead to an exit.)

Roller coaster!

I'm no chicken when it comes to roller coasters. The bigger the better. I'll take the first car any day. Strap me in, send me rolling.

Uncle Trevor, not so much. He got this funny pinched look on his face. "Keep your arms and legs inside the car at all times," he said. **Okay, Mom.**

The biggest roller coaster I ever rode was at the state fair. It was as tall as a skyscraper, with a gigantic vertical drop in the beginning and a good stretch of corkscrews. It was called the Ultimate Roller Coaster 'cause there was no roller coaster better than that one.

But the Ultimate Roller Coaster had nothing on those mining tracks.

Of course, on ACTUAL roller coasters the tracks don't just **STOP** in the middle with nothing under them. Talk about a leap! I was flying.

It. Was. Awesome.

As for Trevor and Hannah—they crashed through a wall at the end. Some people just can't handle a good ride.

Rubies! Emeralds! Diamonds! feldspar?

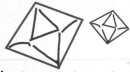

On the other side of the wall Trevor broke through there turned out to be a cave. I stepped through the hole. At first, all I saw was this red glow, like lava. But it wasn't molten-hot like lava. And it wasn't trying to bury us alive like lava. What it was were these red rubies, glowing all over the walls. The walls were MADE of rubies. **Crazy!**

The next cave was full of emeralds. **crazier!**

Uncle Trevor was **psyched** when he saw the next cave was full of **feldspar.** In other words, regular old rock. **The stuff that gets that guy excited . . .**

Then we came to the room with the diamonds. Walls made of diamonds. Ceiling made of diamonds. **The floor we were walking** on . . . **diamonds.** Trevor got all science geek for a second and figured out that we'd wandered into some kind of volcanic tube, which forms crystals like this. Magma must have pushed the crystals up to the surface. So, following that logic, we must be close to the crater. As in, a way to escape. (If you're ever trapped in a volcano, it's helpful to have a science geek around.)

But when I saw the room full of diamonds, this is what was running through my head:

FACT: We are lost inside a volcano.
FACT: It is possible we are never getting out.
FACT: If we DO get out, a few of these diamonds could snag me a Maserati.

Hey, I turn sixteen in a few years. I want to be prepared.

I collected a boatload of diamonds. Well, as much as I could fit in my backpack and then some. One was bigger than my fist. I was trying to pull this one really huge diamond out of the floor when there was a weird sound.

Like this:

crrrrrrr eeeeeeeee aaaaaaaaaa cccck.

Uh-oh.

Muscovite

The stuff under our feet that cracked every which way? It turned out to be a very, very thin rock called **muscovite**. Standing on muscovite is like trying to stand on a piece of glass. It turns out Trevor knows all about muscovite. **Too bad he didn't tell us about it sooner.**

So we had to be really, really careful about how we moved and where we put our weight. Actually, we really shouldn't have been standing on that muscovite at all.

We started walking out of the cave as lightly as was humanly possible.

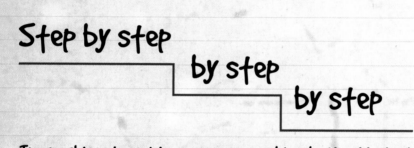

Step by step by step by step

The cracking stopped. I was sure we would make it outta that cave just fine.

Then—JUST MY LUCK—one of the diamonds I swiped took a nose dive out of my backpack. NOOOOOOOOOOOOOOOOOOOOOOOOOO!

I swear, it was like slow motion. I was watching that diamond fall for years. When it landed it just sort of made this little *clink*. And nothing happened. I could breathe again.

Of course, that's when the muscovite cracked open for real and we all fell through.

And I thought the last fall was a long one!

No, this one kept going and going. We screamed. And screamed. We finally stopped screaming. But then we realized we were still falling. So we started screaming again.

Time for Some Yo-Yo

I'm taking a break from falling endlessly into the abyss for some cool yo-yo tricks, courtesy of my dad.

Walk the Dog

1. Curl your arm up, holding the yo-yo close against your ear.

2. Snap your elbow down, letting go of the yo-yo so it swings out away from your hand.

3. Lower the yo-yo till it just about touches the floor.

4. The yo-yo will idle there a sec and then start walking forward like a dog.

5. When your dog gets tired (or the yo-yo falls flat), jerk it back.

Shoot the Moon

(I hit myself in the head with the yo-yo two out of five times with this one. Need more practice.)

1. Fling that yo-yo straight out in front of you.

2. When the yo-yo flies back, don't let yourself catch it. Instead, fling it straight up.

3. When it comes down, don't catch it again—fling it straight out in front of you again.

4. Then catch it. (If you haven't knocked yourself in the chin, do it again.)

The Sleeper Trick

(Here's an easy one. So easy an albino dinosaur could do it.)

1. Hold the yo-yo to your shoulder, palm down and elbow out in front of you.

2. Quickly pull your arm forward and down, flipping your hand upside down. Be smooth about it, and the yo-yo should dangle to the floor. (If you're falling through an abyss while doing this trick and can't _see_ the floor, just let it dangle as far as it goes.)

3. Do not move your hand. Let your yo-yo spin around lazily on the string. It'll sleep like a baby till you break it from its nap and give it a tug to pull it back up.

Water Slide Water Slide Water Slide

That tunnel we were falling down went on for **hundreds of miles.** Maybe thousands. Maybe hundreds of thousands. I never paid attention in science class, so I have no idea how deep a tunnel like that could be.

Uncle Trevor said it had to end. "We'd hit bottom sometime," he said.

Jules Verne or no Jules Verne, what I wanted to know was what was on the bottom? A sea of **boiling-hot lava? Man-eating spiders?** A **pit of snakes?** **Cocoa Pebbles?** I mean, seriously, what were we gonna land on?

Trevor had this theory—the guy eats theories for breakfast—that yadda yadda the sides of the tunnel blah blah blah could have been eroded by water. What he meant in English is that the endless tunnel we were falling through could turn itself into a water slide.

So I focused on that. Water slide. <u>That</u> was the theory I liked.

I looked down and thought maybe there would be water down there if I wanted it bad enough. So I said it under my breath, just said it and said it:

Water Slide Water Slide Water Slide Water Slide Water Slide
Water Slide Water Slide Water Slide Water Slide Water Slide
Water Slide Water Slide Water Slide Water Slide Water Slide
Water Slide Water Slide Water Slide Water Slide Water Slide
Water Slide Water Slide Water Slide Water Slide Water Slide
Water Slide Water Slide Water Slide Water Slide Water Slide
Water Slide Water Slide Water Slide Water Slide Water Slide
Water Slide Water Slide Water Slide Water Slide Water Slide
Water Slide Water Slide Water Slide Water Slide Water Slide
Water Slide Water Slide Water Slide Water Slide Water Slide
Water Slide Water Slide Water Slide Water Slide Water Slide
Water Slide Water Slide Water Slide Water Slide Water Slide
Water Slide Water Slide Water Slide Water Slide Water Slide
Water Slide Water Slide Water Slide Water Slide Water Slide
Water Slide Water Slide Water Slide Water Slide Water Slide
Water Slide Water Slide Water Slide Water Slide.

And what d'ya know . . . My wish came true.

The tunnel filled with water and we shot through it. I just remember being completely soaked all of a sudden. Hardly able to see a thing. Sliding everywhere. Then *SPLOOSH.*

That's when everything went blue.

Electric Birds. Enough Said.

Here's where this journal is gonna start sounding more scientific. (Man, I should've used graph paper.) Anyway, I'll just write down what I saw. No opinions. No making fun of Trevor. And no doodles in the margins.

I saw:

1. Blue, glowing birds—they looked electric, like crosses between bluebirds and fireflies. There were thousands of them. I named them glowbirds, so if that's ever in a science book I should get the credit.

And not just that, but a whole entire world under the Earth's crust. As in:

2. A real, flowing waterfall. (The lagoon it was filling was what broke our fall.)

3. Ferns as tall as pine trees.

4. Gigantic, almost neon-colored flowers. (Dude, I swear the ones that looked like mutant daisies were taller than my house.)

5. Mountains. Yes, actual mountains UNDER THE SURFACE OF THE EARTH.

6. A sky filled with glowing electricity, bright as day, so it looked like it was crowded with millions of intensely bright stars.

7. Eighty-two degrees down there, like the best part of summer vacation.

So all this convinced me that *Journey to the Center of the Earth* by Jules Verne was no book of science fiction—it was genuine FACT. Verne had described this place in his book, and here it was. This proved that Hannah's dad, who had been locked up in a loony bin for talking about this place, hadn't been crazy after all. It proved that Trevor hadn't been wasting his life studying these theories.

It also proved that Max Anderson—my dad—was right, too.

But Those Weren't Trees.

There was this guy in the Jules Verne book named Lidenbrock. I'll call him L.B. L.B. was the guy who made it down here. Maybe he was a real person. Maybe L.B. made it out of this place alive and told Jules Verne all about it so he could write it down and tell the whole world. L.B., I was rooting for him. If he could make it out, so would we.

We walked around for a while, just in this daze. But I was starving, and since I didn't see a hotdog cart anywhere, we hit the trees to split up the few fruit bars Hannah had brought with her. Except the trees weren't trees. They were fossilized mushrooms. ENORMOUS fossilized mushrooms.

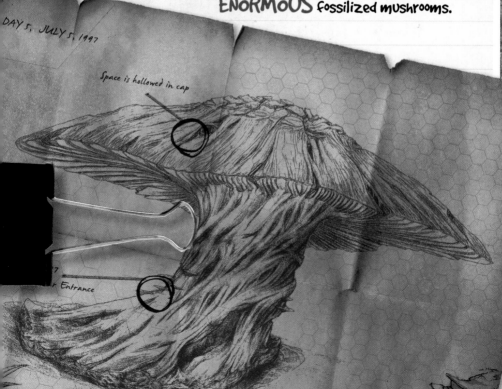

DAY 5, JULY 5, 1997

Space is hollowed in cap

r Entrance

I forgot the fruit bars and kept walking. The mushrooms' skin felt rough and hard, like tree bark. Then I saw something even weirder in the distance. There was a hole in one of the mushrooms. It was tall enough for a person to fit through. Actually, it sort of looked like a doorway.

Then I realized what it was: a house.

Somebody actually lived there. In the GIANT mushroom.

Trevor and Hannah came running. What we found was this mushroom hut. Inside was someone's old **camping equipment**, an old kerosene lamp, ANCIENT stuff. Pre-batteries ancient. Like, from the 1800s.

L.B.!

I found this stack of paper that looked like dried leaves or something. L.B. must have been desperate for paper. Buried in there was this dusty old notebook. Somebody's top-secret journal, no doubt. I opened it up immediately. (Like you didn't do the same to read this.)

AT EITHER RELATIVELY LOW PRESSURE
IN THE SPINEL STABILITY FIELD—
OR AT HIGHER PRESSURES
IN THE GARNET STABILITY FIELD.

The notebook was filled with these scientific notes I couldn't for the life of me figure out. And, like, graphs and stuff, and also some hand-drawn maps. One map showed that there was an ocean nearby.

I was positive now—this was L.B.'s notebook! I waved it in Trevor's face.

Uncle Trevor's eyes bugged out.

"That's Lindenbrock's notebook," he said.

"But that's not Lidenbrock's handwriting," he said.

And I looked down.

Trevor opened his copy of *Journey to the Center of the Earth*, the one he took from my dad's box of stuff. And he held the pages next to each other so we could compare the handwriting.

That notebook had my dad's handwriting in it. Maybe L.B. had been here once. But my dad had been here, too.

Some Stuff About Dad

I'm not gonna talk about how Hannah found my dad's body. How we had to bury him.

No.

But I don't know what to say.

The thing is, I barely knew my dad. I saw pictures. I heard stories that other people told me. He was this smart, important scientist. He was brave. I heard that all the time—everyone always said that. But, as I said, he disappeared when I was a little. I never got the **CHANCE** to know him for myself. Would he have played basketball with me? Would he have gone on the Ultimate Roller Coaster with me fifty times in one day? You know, I wondered about the daily stuff you have no way of knowing when you don't know your dad. But seeing this place he believed in, making it down there, knowing for a fact that he was right, had been right all along . . . Maybe in a little way it was sort of like I did know him, just a little better than before.

This is from my dad's journal. Trevor let me keep it.

↓

August 14th, 1997

I thought I could surprise Trevor and the rest of the world with my discovery, but I've been stuck down here for six weeks. I miss my wife, my brother, and I miss my baby boy. If I don't make it out, I will have lost out on the greatest discovery of all—seeing the man my son would grow up to become.

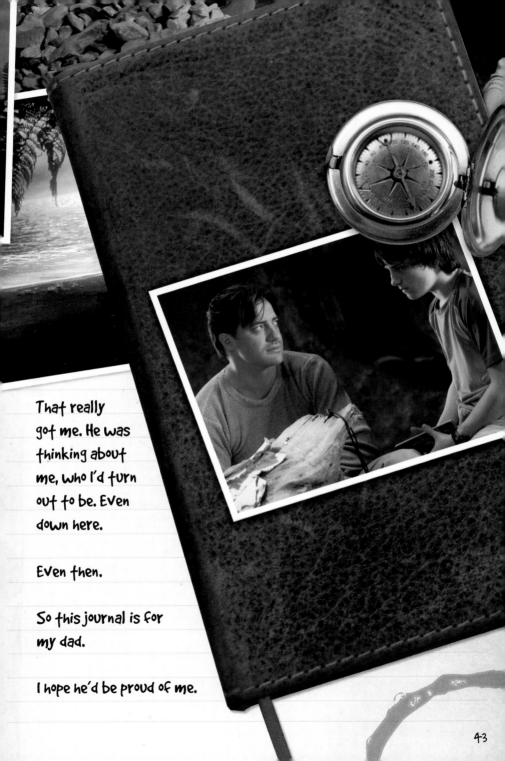

That really
got me. He was
thinking about
me, who I'd turn
out to be. Even
down here.

Even then.

So this journal is for
my dad.

I hope he'd be proud of me.

Hot Pocket (minus the pepperoni)

What we learned was that my dad made it down there, but for some reason he didn't make it out. That's what was so hard to face.

Uncle Trevor and Hannah combed through my dad's journal, looking for clues about what happened and if he had figured out a way back up to the surface.

I let them look. I was trying not to think too much about my dad, but I couldn't help it. Also, it was hot, and getting hotter. And there were these little shakes, or tremors, like tiny little earthquakes every once in a while. I stretched out in what had been my dad's hammock and closed my eyes for a few minutes.

Trevor and Hannah **thought** I was taking a nap. Really, I was just listening to every single thing they were saying. (Suckers!)

Trevor was telling Hannah that my dad's notes said it was supposed to be just seventy-five degrees down there. It was way hotter than that. My dad had this whole diagram in his notebook. Trevor told Hannah that it looked like the Earth split open. You could see all these little tubes running through it. Air pockets, Trevor called them. He said we were in one right now. An air pocket surrounded by molten-hot lava.

So what happens when you're sitting around minding your own business in an air pocket surrounded by molten lava? Well, it heats up. Like an oven. The temperature could reach two hundred degrees.

And what happens to things that reach two hundred degrees? They **boil.**

I wanted out.

I got up off the hammock. I asked Trevor what we should do. He said my dad had come up with an escape plan, but he'd obviously run out of time before he could escape. Hannah said, "Your dad didn't make it, so why should we follow his plan?"

I'll tell you why: My dad was right about how to get down here. I knew, I just <u>knew</u>, he would be right about how to get back up.

Topside vs. Center of the Earth

No way was I staying down there under the Earth for a minute longer than we had to. I wanted to go topside, to the surface, where trees are trees and not mushrooms, where my mom was, where it wasn't so insanely hot. I mean, I knew it was Jules Verne's world and all, like I was witnessing some scientific miracle... material for term papers for <u>years</u>... but still. Topside vs. the center of the Earth. It was no contest.

Topside	Center of the Earth
Grilled hamburger	Grilled trilobite
Seventy-five degrees and cloudy	Sweltering heat like the inside of an oven
Watching TV	Watching the walls of the enormous mushrooms
Starry skies	Gassy sky that only looks like it's filled with stars
Pigeons	Glowbirds (Center of the Earth wins there)

Like I said, no contest.

North Is South and South Is North.

We decided to follow my dad's escape plan. We had his map with all these lines running across it—lines this way, lines that way. Really, all I cared about was the ocean that would lead us to that river. (Yes, an actual ocean. Underground. Believe it.) We needed a boat or something to get across, and we needed that boat right away. One minute it's ninety-five degrees, next minute it's close to one hundred.

Trevor and Hannah built a raft. They made a sail that would act as a kite. I had some grilled trilobite. Tasty. Then we were off. Trevor gave me a compass. It was my dad's. Trevor found it down there. It was a normal metal compass, with scratch marks all over it, as if my dad were constantly dropping it. To most people, a piece of junk. But not to me.

I have this real fuzzy memory. My dad was showing me how a compass works. I think it was this compass—it had to be. I remember the numbers on it. He told me to hold on to it. And then he picked me up and spun me around in circles. The needle went around and around. I thought it was a toy. You know, a game, just this thing you do that doesn't mean anything.

But that compass went with my dad around the world. It went with him down there. So, I figured, I'm gonna use it. Didn't remember exactly **HOW** to use the thing. (There was more to it than spinning in circles.) But Trevor reminded me that down under the Earth's crust the polarity is reversed. North is south down there. South is north.

So we had to sail north across the sea to get to the river. That meant we had to sail south. (Though, really, we were going north.) I tried not to think too hard about it.

We got in the raft and put the kite up so the wind could pull us.

The ocean was nothing like the ocean I'm used to. When you go to the Atlantic Ocean on the Jersey Shore, you see a boardwalk and a bunch of babies eating sand. When you look out into the distance you see the water, yeah, but you also see boats, and buoys, and lights. There are hints of civilization everywhere. I mean, it's the ocean, sure, but you always remember that you're in New Jersey. Down there, Jules Verne's ocean? Just water. Endless water. It sorta freaked me out.

But then a glowbird started following us. I liked the extra company.

49

Never Enough Adventure!

At some point the winds started to pick up. We got caught in a storm. Plus it was one hundred and fourteen degrees by then, and climbing.

Trevor looked over at me and said, "Hey, Sean, enough adventure for you yet?" Like he thought I wouldn't be able to handle it. I sure showed him.

Speaking of, if he thinks I'm done after this trip, he's dead wrong.

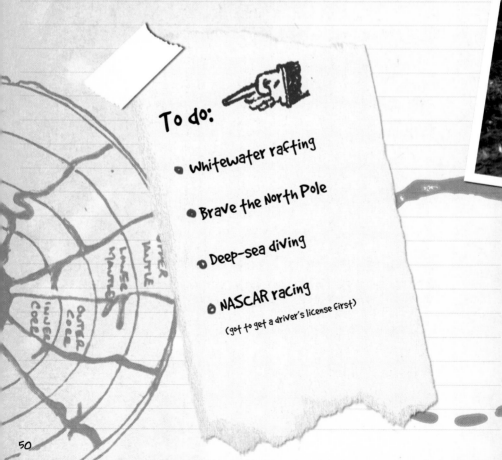

To do:

- Whitewater rafting

- Brave the North Pole

- Deep-sea diving

- NASCAR racing
  (got to get a driver's license first)

And, of course, the most obvious:
Climb to the top of Mount Everest.

I have plans to make it up there one day soon, without letting any of my toes freeze off. It'll take a while to convince my mom. I wonder if she'll think I'm old enough next year, when I turn fourteen.

51

Attack of the Prehistoric Fish

Something was moving down there in the water under the raft. It was blurry, glowing a little. Trevor said it was just plankton. Man, was he wrong.

It was too big to be plankton. I knew it was some kind of fish. So I leaned in, took a closer look. I was thinking maybe it was some funny-looking trout; maybe they have hands and feet down under the surface of the Earth, I don't know. Or, even better, a glowing dolphin! No such luck.

The fish was huge. The fish was huger than huge. The fish tried to bite off my whole head. That thing was prehistoric—the kind of prehistoric that makes you want to run.

And to top it all off, the fish brought friends!

(The big guy was hungry.)

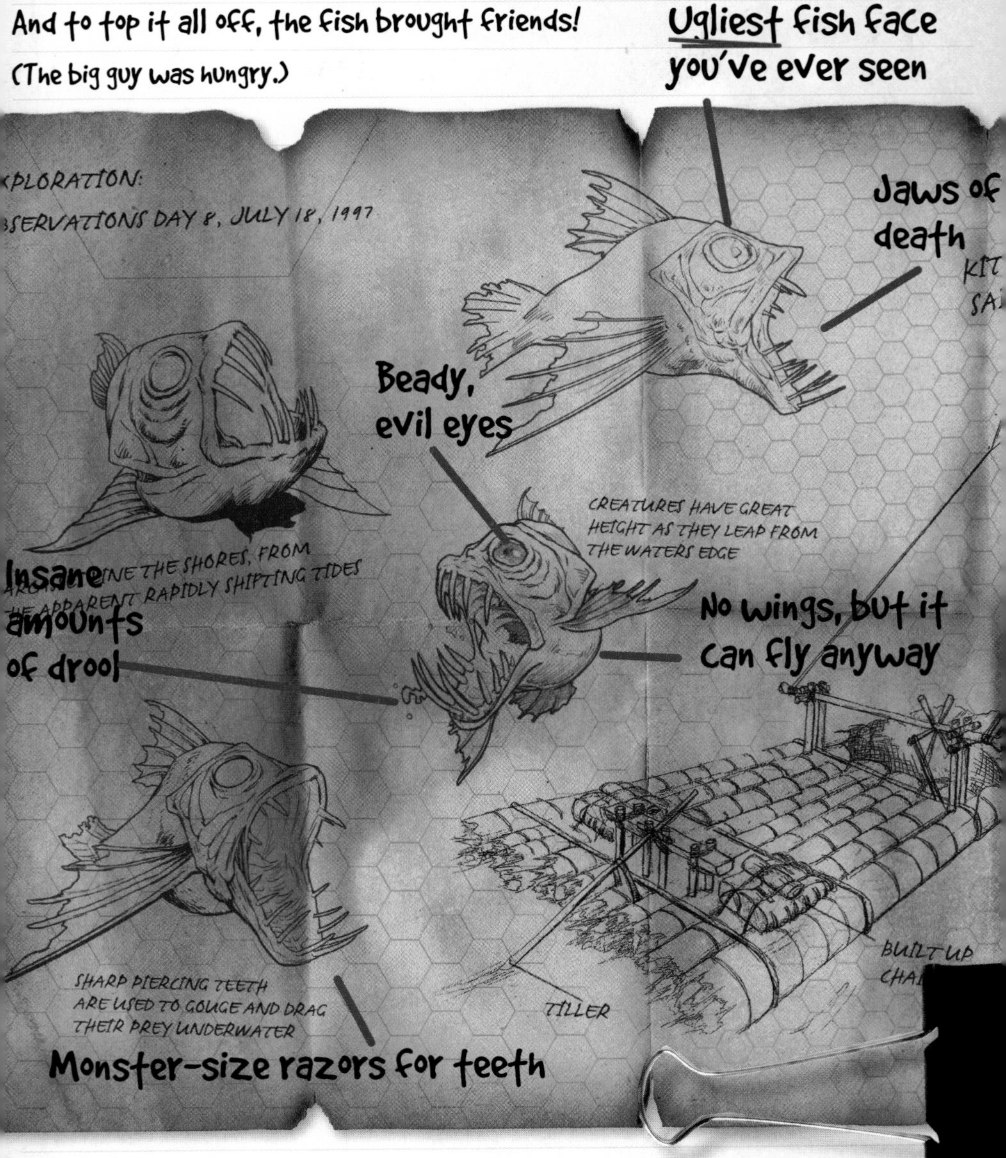

Ugliest fish face you've ever seen

Jaws of death

KIT
SA

EXPLORATION:

OBSERVATIONS DAY 8, JULY 18, 1997

Beady, evil eyes

CREATURES HAVE GREAT HEIGHT AS THEY LEAP FROM THE WATERS EDGE

Insane amounts of drool

...INE THE SHORES, FROM ...APPARENT RAPIDLY SHIPTING TIDES

No wings, but it can fly anyway

SHARP PIERCING TEETH ARE USED TO GOUGE AND DRAG THEIR PREY UNDERWATER

TILLER

BUILT UP
CHA

Monster-size razors for teeth

53

Can You Hear Me Now?

So there we were, in the middle of the Attack of the Monster Fish, when I heard this weird sound. Like a ringtone. Like the ringtone from **my** cell phone. Huh?

It was Mom.

We had a really awful connection—even worse than when you're in an elevator. She wanted to know where Uncle Trevor and I were and, what with all the **splashing** going on (one of the monster fish was trying to bite Hannah). I just said the first thing that came to me: **a fishing trip.**

I could have said a ton of other things. Playing video games. At a **baseball game. Cleaning the garage.**
Disneyland!

But it didn't matter. It's not like she'd ever guess the truth.

Still, I needed her to know that I was okay. I tried to tell her (while fighting a monster fish at the same time), but the fish was in one hand and the phone was in the other, **and before I knew it . . .**

...SPLASH.

The monster fish knocked my phone into the water.

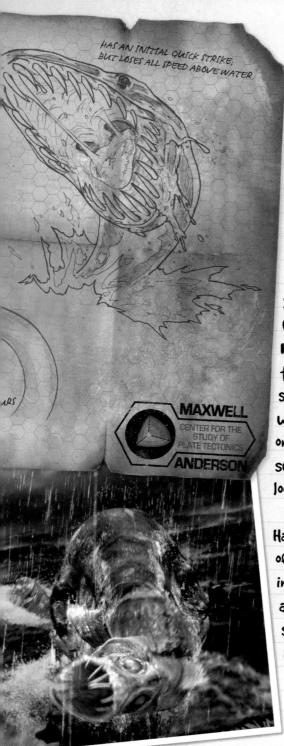

HAS AN INITIAL QUICK STRIKE, BUT LOSES ALL SPEED ABOVE WATER

MAXWELL
CENTER FOR THE
STUDY OF
PLATE TECTONICS
ANDERSON

Go Fly a Kite

There were a few more fish attacks, but then this **gigantic ugly sea serpent** (and when I say ugly, I mean ugly) started going after the fish himself. Thanks, guy. Glad he wanted his dinner, because that sure saved us.

Still, **that wasn't the end of the prehistoric monsters.** I just remember the lightning flashes. The serpents shooting out of the water. Trying to keep an eye on our kite in the sky. Then one serpent knocked our kite line loose. Trevor grabbed it.

Hannah grabbed the other line of the kite, trying to keep it up in the air. I manned the tiller and steered us away from the serpents, and Trevor tied off his rope, keeping us in line.

We were free and clear. It was all good. (Not.)

There was this huge gust of wind, and before we knew it the kite line got yanked out of Hannah's hands. She screamed and let go. Trevor went for her, while I grabbed the rope and tried to hold on tight. Maybe I held on too tight, because one second I was in the boat with Hannah and Trevor keeping the kite in the sky . . .

And the next second I was IN THE SKY <u>with</u> the kite.

<u>Hanging</u> from the kite.

I never want to go fishing again. Plus, kites? Got a bit of a phobia now.

I don't know how long I was up in the air. I remember looking down, **far down**. Seeing the boat. Seeing Hannah. Seeing Trevor . . . then seeing **nothing**, just stars. I guess that's when I blacked out.

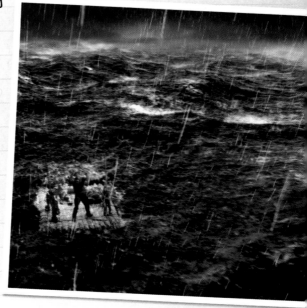

Me No Speak Jurassic

Next thing I knew, I came to. I could feel sand underneath me, wet sand. I was drenched. I tried to move. I still had my legs, my arms—but every single thing on me was hurting, like I got slammed, which I guess maybe I did. My tongue was just this dry wasteland. I was so thirsty I would have sucked down a gallon of prune juice.

I tried to open my eyes. I just saw blackness, like there was a blindfold over my face. It took so much effort to get my eyes open. One eye—I could see only this blurry whiteness, sort of sharp-looking. Cliffs? Mountains? Both eyes open. Okay, it looked like something white, with really sharp edges. Lots of them. It was very close to my face. It took some more seconds for both my eyes to focus.

AGCKK.

I had my face inches away from a giant dead fish, its jaws gaping wide open like it had been just about to eat me before it croaked. Just the thing I want to see when I first wake up.

I sat up. I was on a beach. The ocean was straight ahead of me—empty. Trevor and Hannah were nowhere in sight. Neither was our raft. I was on my own in the middle of nowhere. Great.

I tried to think. We had a plan. Head north. or was it south? North. South. North. South. **NORTH**.

That was the plan. Head north. I knew that was where Trevor and Hannah were headed, so I'd just meet up with them there. They probably figured I fell off the kite and was swallowed by a prehistoric whale. Well, it would be a nice surprise when they saw me.

I started walking. Then I saw a light. It was my little buddy, Glowbird. He must have been following me all along. He started chirping at me. He seemed to think we were having a deep conversation, but I couldn't understand a word. Sorry, guy. I don't speak Jurassic.

But he kept chirping. He flew away from the shore, then turned back and looked at me. He wanted me to follow. Glowbird was saving my life.

Magnetic Rock-Hopping

The big thing in my gym class back home—what we'd look forward to all year instead of the usual dodgeball or kickball—was the obstacle course. You'd go through it as fast as you could: climb the rope, hop the pommel horse, jump through the tires, run to the finish. You'd get your time, and whoever made it to the end fastest won. Not once in gym class was there danger of falling off the tire course into a bottomless abyss. Good thing I could handle those tires, though—that skill would come in handy in a minute.

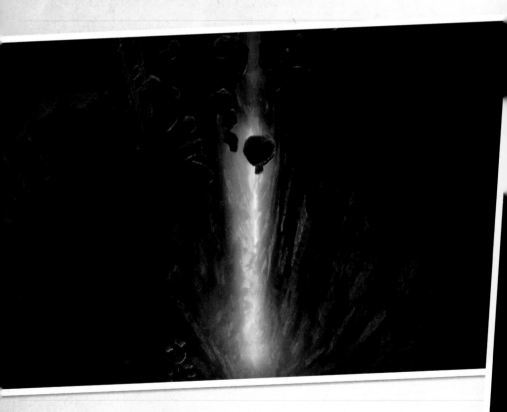

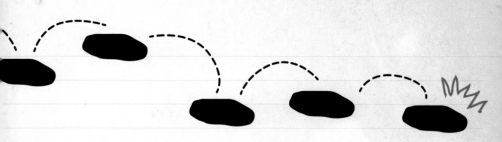

Glowbird led me where I needed to go. First to a river of fresh water so I could get something to drink, and then due north (south according to the compass) to the river where I was hoping I'd meet up with Trevor and Hannah, as planned.

That's when we came to the obstacle course. No tires on the ground here. These were rocks that were floating in midair. **Magnetic rocks.**

It was like a path of stones through the air. I stepped from one to the next. Sounds easy. Except when you look down and see that the stones are floating magnetically in place with nothing below them for <u>hundreds of feet</u>.

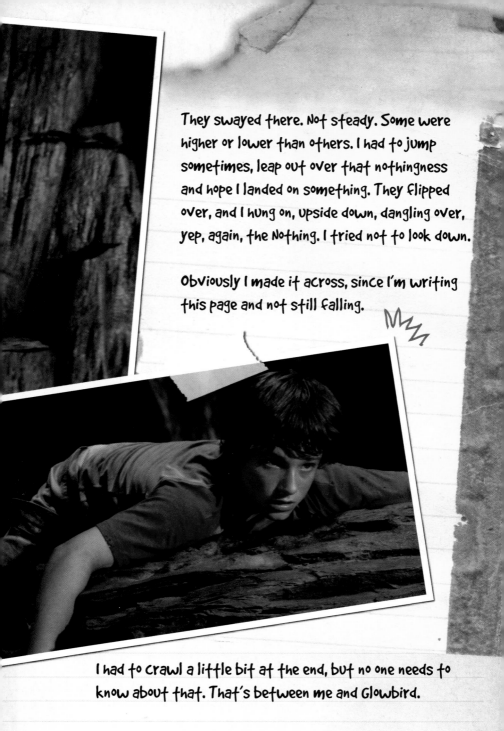

They swayed there. Not steady. Some were higher or lower than others. I had to jump sometimes, leap out over that nothingness and hope I landed on something. They flipped over, and I hung on, upside down, dangling over, yep, again, the Nothing. I tried not to look down.

Obviously I made it across, since I'm writing this page and not still falling.

I had to crawl a little bit at the end, but no one needs to know about that. That's between me and Glowbird.

The Largest Predatory Dino That Ever Lived.

(No Joke.)

Glowbird had my <u>back</u>. I just wish the little guy knew to keep a lookout for dinosaurs.

So, before this "vacation" with Uncle Trevor, the most I knew about dinosaurs was from a trip to the Museum of Natural History when I was a kid. Bones, that's what I remember, a load of honking big bones. Dinosaurs are much scarier when they've got skin on.

But first, the bones.

A field of them.

Me and Glowbird were heading south (north) over a field of white rocks. Or I thought they were rocks. But then I realized that this one half-buried boulder looked weirdly like a head. **A big dino head.** And so it was: There was a skull . . . some rib bones . . . oh. I'd just wandered past a giant dinosaur skeleton.

Well, at least it's dead. That's what I thought to myself.

Till I heard the ROAR.

Dinosaur two! In living color! Alive and giving chase!

Well, not really <u>**color**</u>—the big guy was an albino. Plus, he wasn't exactly "giving chase" at first. He was just sitting there. Towering over me. And drooling. A huge glob of dinosaur spit dropped down on me from the sky. I wasn't sure if I was more grossed out or scared. (Scared.)

What do you do when standing over you is an albino Gigantosaurus, the biggest predatory dinosaur that ever lived? You run. No shame in running.

And then, when the Gigantosaurus keeps coming, claws out, jaws open? **You hide.** No shame in that, either.

one Last Yo-Yo Trick

Recap:

Giant albino dinosaur chasing me. Check.

Hiding behind a rock so said albino dinosaur doesn't eat me. (Check.)

Too much excitement for you? Let's take a yo-yo break. You can yo-yo anywhere, really. You can yo-yo while hiding in a cave with an albino dinosaur roaring outside about how much he wants to eat you. You'd be <u>insane</u> to yo-yo at a time like that, but technically you <u>could</u>, if you wanted to.

So this one's called
Around the World

1. Wind up the yo-yo tightly and hold it firmly in the palm of your hand.

2. Throw the yo-yo out in front of you like you did during the Sleeper trick.

3. While the yo-yo is still sleeping, swoop your arm backward in a circle, keeping your palm facing the ceiling. The yo-yo should swing in an arc backward over your head in a full circle.

4. Circle it around a few times.

5. Grab it out of the air and hold it back in your palm.

6. Then, if there's an albino dinosaur breathing down your neck . . . RUN.

What, Haven't You Ever Seen an Albino Dinosaur Before?

Back to the Valley of Bones, where my new friend, the most enormous dinosaur I've ever seen, was trying to shove his big head into the cave where I was hiding. Talk about teeth. The guy had more than I could count. And sharp ones, like razors. But worse was his breath. Down under the crust of the Earth they were in desperate need of mouthwash.

I backed up against the far wall of the cave. His jaws were inches away. There was nowhere for me to go. That's when I heard my name. Was I hearing voices? Did I think the dinosaur was TALKING to me now?

Oh. It was just Uncle Trevor.
UNCLE TREVOR!!!

He was on the other side of the rock wall, pulling out the stones to make a hole big enough for me to escape. Somehow, in seconds, he did. He pulled me out. He saved my life. Sure, it was _his_ fault we were down there running from dinosaurs, but I'm not the kind of guy to hold a grudge. He did save my life, even if he almost got me eaten first. I sure was happy to see the guy. He was happy to see me, too. (Yeah yeah, we hugged, okay, move on.) Then Trevor looked up and saw my albino pal.

"What is that?" he said.

"Haven't you ever seen an albino dinosaur before?" I said. **Then we ran.**

We headed for the river. Trevor said that Hannah had gone to find her way to the surface—he wanted her to get out. But I didn't believe it. She wouldn't just leave us down there.

That's when we came to this patch of muscovite, the flimsy rock we fell through the last time. Trevor pushed me away. He said, "Go, get to the river."

I just remember watching Trevor run. The Gigantosaurus was chasing him. There was my uncle, running faster than I've ever known a human being could run, and the albino monster hot on his heels, and Trevor crying about how he never should have left his lab and fieldwork sucks, and then **CRACK**—the muscovite was giving out. Trevor was scrambling. Beneath him was just air. He was gonna fall, _please don't let him fall_. . . The crack was **enormous**. The ground completely vanished. And the Gigantosaurus was falling down into the abyss. Trevor was okay.

Dinosaurs, take a lesson: Don't mess with Uncle Trevor.

The Greatest Mountain Guide on the Planet

Normally we would have taken a moment to celebrate defeating the dinosaur. I mean, it's not every day you meet a walking, breathing, roaring, attacking dinosaur, let alone get the chance to run screaming from one. Seriously. But I guess that's why I'm writing this journal, to remember things like that. Even if it takes me the rest of my life.

Everything was happening so quickly. What I remember after the dinosaur chase is that we felt this tremor under our feet and the ground began to shake. All this steam was shooting out of a nearby cave. Could that be where the water was? Yes! The river! We ran for it. But when we got closer to the water, we realized it was boiling hot. But we had to get down that river to get to the geyser that would shoot us up out of the volcano and to the surface. We needed a boat. A log. Anything that could float. I looked around the cave. Nothin'.

That's when Hannah showed up. And talk about a boat—she was floating on the water in a dinosaur skull. (Way to recycle.) But seriously, no joke on Hannah: That woman is the greatest mountain guide on the planet. We jumped into the skull. I took a seat by the eye socket and we were on our way.

Problem is . . . it was hot. So hot, I'm sweating just writing about it. Hang on, I'm having flashbacks. I'm gonna shove my head in the freezer.

Back.

So we were in the skull boat, riding along in a boiling river, when *BUMP*, we hit the bottom of the river. The water was drying up. Our skull boat skidded and threw us down a vertical tunnel. We were stuck in the rocks, and down below us was this weird orange light.

It was magma rising up toward us. We were goners. There was supposed to be water in the tunnel, water that would shoot us up to the surface. **THAT WAS THE WAY OUT.**

But we were too late. We had missed the geyser.

We had two options:

1. Climb out of the tunnel and sit there waiting to get baked like a barbecue-flavored potato chip in the hot, hot sun.

or

2. Stay in the tunnel and sit there waiting for an up-close-and-personal introduction to the boiling hot lava. Hey, lava. How you doin'? Here, eat my face.

Choices, choices.

I'm not gonna say I doubted my dad's escape plan at that moment, that I doubted Uncle Trevor or Hannah or the cushy dinosaur-head cruise liner we were riding in, or that I doubted Jules Verne.

But I did have some doubts. That's only human.

Skull Ride

So there we were. Hot as a pepperoni sizzling in a pizza oven.

All Trevor said was that we were too late. Without water, he said, there was no steam. Without steam, we're not going anywhere.

That's when I noticed that the walls of the cave were **wet.**

"Impossible," Trevor said.
But it was wet—water tends to do that. Plus, it was cold.

There's water behind the wall! Trevor was suddenly yelling. It was a pocket, he said. The walls were lined with magnesium. Then Trevor and Hannah got out the flares. I remembered what happened the last time Trevor was near magnesium:

Explosion! That was just what we needed. It could cause the water behind it to come rushing out, to hit the lava and make a geyser. And that would shoot us up to the surface.

We had only three flares left. Three chances to get out.

Trevor tried the first one, hurling it straight at the magnesium. But the flare fell into the pool of lava. Lava: 1. Trevor: 0.

He tried the second flare and missed. By a mile. Lava: 2. Trevor: 0.

Trevor wouldn't take the chance with the last flare. We had to get him closer to the magnesium. So we tied some rope around Trevor's feet. Lowered the guy down headfirst.

He banged the flare on the wall. Nothing. We were trying to hold him, but it was hard. My arms were shaking. Bang, bang, bang. Nothing.

Hot, burning air whipped at us. It was so hot I couldn't breathe. And Trevor was banging and I was choking and his legs were slipping and then *BANG!* The magnesium caught fire. White light exploded down in the tunnel.

We pulled Trevor up just in time. There was this enormous *BOOM* and the wall broke open and water exploded through.

It shot through the wall like a hundred fire hoses straight at the lava. Then, a huge ball of steam shot up at us and we were zoomed up in the geyser. The skull rode up and up on the rising steam. The force plastered us to the bottom of the skull. The heat was suffocating. The noise was incredible. Seriously, you had to be there.

Then I saw it. This blue speck up above us. It was getting bigger, closer. Was that . . . the sky?

It was. Blue sky at long last.

What Happens in the Center of the Earth Stays in the Center of the Earth.

We blasted out of the volcano into the blue sky, our skull boat moving like a rocket ship. We soared. We shot up through the clouds. We were out, out at last. Score!

Then we started to fall back down. And fast. Sometimes I forget the stuff from science class, you know: what comes up must come down? Or is that from a song? Anyway, we did.

BAM!

The skull smacked down on the side of some mountain. Then we were skating down the mountainside like a blind bobsledder. Fun in theory. Freaky in reality.

I don't know what I was expecting. Just not hundreds of rows of vines filled with . . . grapes. Yup, lots and lots of grapes. We were in a vineyard!

We barreled through those vines, crushing the grapes left and right, smashing the place to a juicy pulp. And then, for good measure, because it's not like our skull boat destroyed enough of the place, we went shooting straight for . . . somebody's house.

That's right. We'd survived killer monster fish, rabid dinosaurs, and boiling lava, and now we were about to be crushed by a **HOUSE**.

oh, the irony.

But the skull was slowing. Somehow, miraculously (if you believe that sort of thing, which I don't, really, I don't, but it was sort of lucky that we slowed just at the moment, not to mention the fact that we got out of the volcano), our skull boat came to a nice solid stop at the front door.

We sat there, staring. We were completely covered in grapes. And behind us, that volcano we shot out of? That was **MOUNT VESUVIUS.**

An old man ran out of the vineyard screaming at us in Italian. I couldn't understand one word, except I knew why he was mad: We'd bulldozed his vineyard. The whole place was ruined.

I had to make it up to him. So I dug around in my backpack and pulled out one of the diamonds. Hey, I just took a few. For geological samples. A few <u>pounds</u> of geological samples. What do you want from me? I'm the son of a scientist.

So I gave the old man one of the diamonds. A nice big one—maybe that would make up for the mess we left him with.

Guess so. The guy got a big smile. Then he said (in English) that we could sled down the other hill if we wanted, no problem.

THE END.

oh, not yet. I still have more to say.

So that's how we made it out of the volcano.

If my mom asks where we went on vacation, Uncle Trevor says I should tell her he took me to Italy. Gotta remember that. I sure did have the most **KILLER** (as in really, really awesome) time of my whole entire life in Italy, um . . . <u>fishing.</u>

Next Up: Atlantis?

Everything in this journal is 100% fact. This is scientific evidence— <u>not</u> science fiction. I should send this in to some museum so scientists can study it and make new theories and kids will go on field trips to come look at these pages and take pictures like they do in the room with all the mummies and I'll probably become famous and everything.

So after we popped out of Mount Vesuvius, things just got better from there, **thanks to me.**

I'm the one who thought ahead and shoved the diamonds in my backpack. Therefore, Trevor and Hannah owe me a huge thanks for the money to get their new volcanology institute going.

AL STUDIES HAVE SHOWN THAT
CONGRUENT MELTING OF AMPHIBOLE
MANTLE PERIDOTITES OR IN
LTRAMAFIC VEIN ASSEMBLAGES CAN
DDUCE NEPHELINE-NORMATIVE LAVAS
EITHER RELATIVELY LOW PRESSURE
THE SPINEL STABILITY FIELD—
AT HIGHER PRESSURES
HE GARNET STABILITY FIELD.

When we got home, Trevor said we should go on vacation again, somewhere different next time. Maybe for two weeks. Maybe during my winter break.

Then he slipped me another book. It was all messed up, the corners of the pages turned down, all these scribbles in the margins. It's called *The Lost City of Atlantis*. I think that means some scuba diving!

Almost forgot, I took one last thing with me from the Center of the Earth. Something better than any diamond . . . Problem is, it flew out of my bag the other day. <u>Literally.</u>

Lost!
Pet Bird

- Blue glowy feathers

- Looks sort of prehistoric

- Chirps a lot

- Answers to the name of Glowbird

So if you see a glow-in-the-dark bird, point him toward Ottawa.